Ready— To Resist

by

Ruth-Anne Mullan

PublishAmerica
Baltimore

© 2006 by Ruth-Anne Mullan.
All rights reserved. No part of this book may be reproduced, stored in a retrieval system or transmitted in any form or by any means without the prior written permission of the publishers, except by a reviewer who may quote brief passages in a review to be printed in a newspaper, magazine or journal.

First printing

All characters appearing in this work are fictitious. Any resemblance to real persons, living or dead, is purely coincidental.

ISBN: 1-4241-4634-8
PUBLISHED BY PUBLISHAMERICA, LLLP
www.publishamerica.com
Baltimore

Printed in the United States of America

*This book is dedicated
To my precious family
Every child, grandchild,
in-law, aunt, uncle, and cousin.
To my sister and her family.
And to my wonderful husband, Gus.*

Chapter 1

Dan threw back the covers determinedly, if a little reluctantly. He reached forward to turn off the alarm as he sat up.

As he was about to enter the bathroom, he remembered. He ran over to the bedroom window and looked out. The street was empty, which wasn't strange at this time of day. There was the red brick house across the street. The profuse ornamentation of showy flowers and concrete garden paraphernalia looked as it always did in the summer. Nothing seemed unusual as far as he could see. He looked up and down the length of the nicely paved street. It must have been a dream. *It was certainly a vivid one,* he thought.

Last night, in what must have been his dream, at about ten o'clock, the news was just coming on. He and probably most of the other residents on the street were settling in to watch it. The power went off! It seemed to be off all over the area. Nothing illuminated the darkness. There didn't seem to be a moon, and only a few stars were visible. After locating the Big Dipper, Dan decided that he might as well go to bed. It was almost time to, anyway. He was sure that the power would come back on in a few minutes, but he was tired. Any news could wait until he heard it over the radio at breakfast.

Dan easily went around the house that had been his home for the last thirty-two years. He had just made a hand banister connection when a loud rumble reached his ears. It seemed to reverberate through his body before he was even aware of hearing it.

Spotlights as well as the lights of multiple vehicles nightmarishly lit up the darkened street and pinpointed spots on the red or yellow brick houses. The ominous procession trekked by. Jeeps, tanks, and trucks that appeared to be full of soldiers eerily rolled slowly down the street. The hair rose on the back of his neck, and his body tensed. His confused mind tried to make sense of a sight that reminded him of the dark drama of a *Batman* cartoon. A loudspeaker began to resound adding to the illusion, relaying a message. "Congratulations, you are now under our control. All of North America has joined the New World government. The world will finally be one. There will be no more wars, famine, or want. Natural resources will be shared, resulting in peace and prosperity for all. We are the policemen of the New World Order, supreme authority in all the cities of the world. We have interrupted your power supply and will restore it to you momentarily. You may follow your usual routine until advised otherwise."

While he was wondering what would have caused a nightmare like that, his eyes took in the familiar room. Once his nursery, it had changed as he grew. His favorite possessions were here. Many of the trophies and pennants he had won either alone or with team effort were displayed on the top shelves of the display unit that took up a whole wall. Baseball, bowling, college football, and, of course, hockey and lacrosse had taken up much of his time as a boy. Some of these pursuits even followed him into his manhood. In addition to these treasures from the past were the current projects and collections that related to his multitude of interests.

He yawned sleepily and stretched before making his way to the bathroom to check himself out in the mirror. He did this ritually, although not from vanity. He was a good-looking guy with wavy black hair. His full lips were shaped in a manner that made it look as though he was on the verge of a smile. A pair of deep blue eyes completed the visage that stared back at him from the mirror. The well-muscled athletic body wasn't visible in the old-fashioned mirror that doubled as the door of the medicine cabinet. He didn't really notice his individual features and didn't worry about his appearance, but was reassured every morning by seeing that he was still himself. Inspection over, he started his morning routine of toilet, shave and shower.

Chapter 2

Clean shaven, dressed, coffee in hand, he opened the front door in order to retrieve his paper from the porch where Alan pitched it every morning. The kid wasn't bad at paper tossing. It usually landed about a foot from the door. He could reach it easily without leaving the doorstep. There was no paper yet, so Dan stepped outside to wait. The boy was punctual. Sure enough, he was just rounding the corner on his bike, paper carrier balanced expertly on the crossbar. Dan watched him toss the papers with practiced accuracy. When the paperboy came closer, Dan expected a smile and wave. He was surprised, though, by the boy's expression. He looked as though he was afraid.

"Soldiers," he whispered, just loud enough for Dan to catch it. "They're around the corner!"

Then, before Dan's eyes, Alan looked up as though listening to something and suddenly, he disappeared.

Dan stared incredulously as the now rider-less bike wheeled erratically along a bit before clanging to the sidewalk. Frantic sounds, cars crashing, glass shattering, and what seemed like dozens of explosions of different magnitudes drew his attention from the slowly spinning front wheel of the bike. Startled, he glanced up to see Margie run out of her house.

"My baby, oh, my baby!" she cried. She dashed across the road in front of a car. The driver appeared to be oblivious of her. He sped right at her, hit her hard, and kept going. The vehicle careened down the slope, went through the stop street, and folded into the Johnsons' house.

Horrible explosions rocked the pavement under Dan's feet. Glass shattered. The shrill screech of tires grabbing at the pavement and decisive thuds from collisions of multiple vehicles versus other solid matter filled the air. The noise was ear-splitting. Even the town's air raid siren was sounding. A plane flew so low overhead on a downward angle that it just cleared the houses. It disappeared from view. The fiery explosion that followed the crash seemed practically simultaneous, and smoke rose blackly from somewhere on one of the streets behind his.

When Dan got to Margie, he knew she was dead. Her head was at a crazy angle, eyes staring at him. He remembered her baby boy and as he heard the voices of others that were coming to help, he left her there and ran into her house to get the infant. He knew that her husband drove transport and wouldn't be home until the weekend. He wondered how to reach her family. What was he to do with a baby until then? He needn't have worried. After checking the whole house over, he discovered that the little one wasn't even there. The way that Margie had run out of the house crying for her baby perplexed him. Could the child have been kidnaped?

Back out on the street, he joined a small crowd that had gathered around the scene. Amazingly, no driver was in the car that had folded into the corner house. There was no blood except what must have been Margie's, and no sign of the involvement of another human. There was a purse on the floor of the car where it had been thrown sometime during the accident.

The Johnsons were nowhere to be seen. The car was blocking their front entrance. He knew them and grew up with them as neighbors and friends of his mother. Dan felt comfortable in going around back. He gave a rap. There was no response. He let himself in. The key was where he expected to find it. It hung on a nail high up on a branch of their cherry tree.

He entered the kitchen and felt reassured. The aromas of toast and coffee permeated the air. The coffeepot was simmering on the stove. The table was set for breakfast, but on closer inspection, he saw that the toast was cold, still sitting in the toaster and this house was also empty. After checking each room, he ran back to the street and stared disbelievingly at the pandemonium that reigned.

Chapter 3

Confusion was everywhere. People were weeping or calling frantically for their children. As he stood staring, Sarah's house burst into flames. At almost the same time, the foreign sounds of machine guns that were at least for now being fired over their heads cut through the hysteria.

"Silence," a strange voice barked, "you will proceed to your community center for instructions!" The orders came over a loudspeaker.

The nightmare army of last night had rounded the corner into plain view. They were every bit as threatening in the stark daylight.

Everyone was motionless, momentarily stunned.

"Now," the voice commanded. "Disobedience will be strictly dealt with." They started to move toward the community center a few blocks away. Numbly, Dan noted Margie's body. No one had thought to cover her up. For a crazy minute, he wondered if she was cold lying there. The whole group walked almost zombie-like past wrecked cars. A few cars were wrapped around poles. Some were scrunched up into other vehicles. It was hard to tell where one ended and the other began. At first he was concerned for the lives of the people that were involved. He was ashamed to realize that he was grateful to see no signs of life in these accidents. He wouldn't have known what to do anyway. Several homes were on fire. The smell of smoke was suspended thickly, trapped in the summer haze. It made his eyes smart, and he heard quite a few people coughing as they fearfully trudged along. When they passed the church, they got another jolt.

"Look at the graves!" Dave burst out.

"Who could have done that?" commented Marion. All who were not in a total state of shock looked over and saw huge mounds of earth piled here and there. As they got closer, they could see that some of the graves had been disrupted.

There wasn't time to analyze the situation because of the general mayhem. Emergency sirens were shrieking within earshot, but none had arrived on this street yet.

A few jeeps, though, had joined the procession and were now herding Dan and his friends and neighbors as though they were animals. This was much worse than what he thought was a dream earlier this morning.

The playing field at the center was filled with men and women, but no children that Dan could see. People were standing or sitting on the edge of the soccer field, bewildered and scared. Soldiers with machine guns stood menacingly among them. The few attempts at brave outbursts from the crowd were silenced immediately by a wave of the gun or the butt of it applied to the back or head.

Again the voice that was becoming too familiar spoke out over the loudspeaker. "Why are there no children? You have been very clever in achieving their exodus. The fires and other diversions that you have obviously started as a cover will be under control before the day is done. The perpetrators of this rebellion will be caught and punished. There was no need. We have come to bring a better life: a peaceful life. Soon we will find these children wherever they are. You forget! We control the entire world."

Dan wondered how they could think that they had spirited away their children. He thought wryly that he hadn't any better explanation.

They were ordered to line up for a census. The room in the building that was used for meetings, weddings and parties had been set up much as it was on voting days. Dan lined up under the appropriate alphabetical letter. When it was his turn, he faced a very ordinary man except for the gun. The man that sat behind the table was small and neatly mustached. He wore a green uniform, pea green, something like the uniform his uncle had worn in the last war. That was the only resemblance to his pleasant, smiling uncle. This man was dour, which added to the apprehension of those who were forced to stand before him.

The grim-faced soldier punched Dan's name, address, phone number, social insurance number, and birth date into a computer. "Go about your normal day, but be home before dark or you have a good chance of being shot," Stone-face instructed him.

Chapter 4

Dan headed towards his store. Everyone that he passed looked to be in the same stunned state as he was. The evidence of accidents and fires were everywhere. There was a terrible stillness in contrast to the clamor of a few hours ago. Not knowing what else to do, he walked the few short blocks to his store. There were papers out front in their usual place by the door. He opened up, and did the ordinary tasks that he had done by rote for the past ten years. The Coca-Cola sign was turned from closed to open. He checked and stocked the coolers with cans and bottles of pop. Coffee and water for tea were made ready. He put a stack of frozen hamburger patties and a box of wieners out to defrost. The vats were filled with strained oil that had been carefully drained and stored at just the right temperature last night. He turned on the heat. Roast beef and ham were brought out and sliced. Lettuce was washed and drained. He made sure that there was plenty of butter and bread ready, and took a rest. He was glad of the chance to do something comforting in its very routine. Working did its therapy, and he was able to begin to think. What was happening was somehow familiar, as if he'd read something like this before. Perhaps it was in a science fiction magazine. Then it popped into his mind.

His mother, before she died, told him that all of the religions of the world and all of the countries would one day join. She told him that when this happened he should make very sure to not let anybody put a mark on him and made him promise. She told him that if any of these things happened during his lifetime, to look in her Bible for answers. Of course he promised her. He loved her very much. He remembered the day that he had promised her as if it were yesterday. She was intense and emotionally charged. She knew that her time was short, and she wanted to make him understand. He hadn't quite.

Her long gray hair was streaked with white. There was no sign of the vibrant chestnut waves that he remembered. Chrissie had been over earlier and had bathed his mother tenderly. She brushed the flowing silvery mane until it shone. He always enjoyed the sight of his mother's hair. It could only be seen that way at bedtime. The rest of the time it was twisted and pinned up. Now it lay loose and spread out over her pillow. Her once sparkling brown eyes were too shiny. The pupils were dilated because of the drugs that had been administered to her. They still didn't completely control the pain. They served only to lessen her agony for a time.

She had often been labeled "religious." She scoffed at this, and said that men had created religion. Religion didn't even enter into what she had. "Why, a person can even brush their teeth religiously," she pointed out. She stated that she just had a relationship with Jesus. She knew him and she loved him. She hadn't insisted that he live according to her beliefs, but certainly taught him right from wrong.

Whatever she had and he knew that she really had something special, she had been a loving, gentle mother. Her wisdom was there for him whenever he told her about some problem. She seldom volunteered any unless he asked. His mother felt that it was important for every person to make their own decisions and exercise free will. Surprisingly, he did ask her things because he desired to know what she thought quite often. Dan found his mother to be extremely intuitive. It seemed that she'd been right about this situation, too.

The bell over the door jingled, and Chrissie came in. She was definitely not her usual bubbly self. Her face was ashen. She perched on the end stool which was a familiar resting place for her. The cute dimpled blonde came in often just to gab. He loved her visits that seemed to shorten his long working days. They had grown up together and were fast friends. When they were children, they spent a lot of time together.

She played baseball with the guys. At first, some of the other kids objected to a girl on their team, but Dan informed them that if she couldn't play, neither would he. It was his bat and catcher's glove. One game was enough to convince them that it was okay. When she came up to bat and connected, the ball disappeared out of sight. She got them a lot of home runs.

Her parents often included him in their outings. They had a big family. Dan, Chrissie and her three brothers—David, Jagger, and Nathan—fished and swam together. They all went to the same schools. Dan's life wasn't lonely because of them.

He had known for a long time that he loved her. He wasn't sure when it happened, but at her wedding, he was silently grieving. When she came back to town after her husband Ralph died, he knew that he would always love her. They had never discussed love or marriage. Their association had been pure friendship. He wondered how she felt about him but didn't want to change their relationship and lose the easy camaraderie that they enjoyed together. He knew that she was still feeling vulnerable.

They talked about everything and always had. He should have told her years ago how his feelings had changed towards her. He almost had, but she started talking about Ralph as if he was the greatest thing that had ever walked up the main street of town. Dan had listened without revealing his own longing for her as she confided in him. He had a hard time acting as her confidante. When she and Ralph were married, he shook hands with the groom and kissed her gently on the cheek. He managed to wish them happiness, and all without the tears that he was afraid might start to flow.

Chrissie came back to town five years later. Her husband had been killed in a plane crash. They hadn't had any children, and she wanted to be back with her family.

He still hadn't revealed how he felt. He worried that she might be spooked by his feelings so soon after her widowhood. If the time ever came that he knew she felt the same as he did, he would be overjoyed, and nothing would stop him from marrying her!

Chapter 5

Jarring him back to the present, Dan became aware that Chrissie was speaking.

"I can't believe what I've seen today. I was walking past the daycare center next door to me. Tonya was bringing her baby in, as usual. I see her every weekday at the same time. We said good morning the way we always do.

"She was carrying her baby up the walk and all of a sudden, it was gone! Right out of her arms! I couldn't believe it!" Chrissie went on breathlessly, "Tonya got hysterical, and then the door of the daycare opened and Jennifer ran out crying. The new girl, Cynthia, ran out behind her and was shocked into immobility. I couldn't understand Jennifer. Bethany, the regular worker, came out, but wouldn't answer me, so I ran in the open door and found the whole place completely empty. No kids at all! There are at least ten by that time of the morning."

"Go on!"

"While we stood there, incredulously, we heard crashing and shouting and things blowing up. It sounded like bedlam," she continued, unconsciously wringing her hands. "We thought that we had been attacked and there was a war starting. Smoke started pouring out of Maisie's bungalow. We ran in to help her. She can't get around too easily anymore. We couldn't find any trace of her!"

"What about Mr. Munroe?" Dan interjected. "Did you check on him?"

"No, I couldn't. His house just—exploded! Where are those babies?" She searched his face earnestly for an answer and not seeing one, she went on talking. "That man accused us of hiding the kids somewhere. How could we have organized anything like that? We didn't even know that we had a problem until last night."

The milk delivery arrived just then and Jeff, who was also Dan's friend, started to unpack his carrier and stock the fridge with butter and milk. Jeff, always laughing and ready to tease, had gotten Dan into a lot of minor trouble when they were kids. Not on purpose, but because he had always been such a little hellion. Dan always had a lot of fun with him. Everybody in this town hung out together. The town was too small to avoid people that you didn't like. Curt nods were exchanged, and no real conversation followed when you passed someone you weren't too fond of. Formal politeness was the normal behavior toward strangers as well. Migrants to the town went through a period of observation, as in many small towns. Only then could the citizens make up their mind whether or not to accept the newcomers. It wasn't often that anyone new came into town, since the silver mine had closed. It was even less often that they stayed.

Jeff didn't greet them normally as he came in. For once he wasn't smiling. He just shot them a meaningful warning look before bending down quickly to his work. With his back to them he hissed, "Watch out, they were right behind me. Let's meet in the cave, after dark."

There was no time for a reply.

The bell on the door rang out cheerfully. It was obviously unaware of whom it was announcing, because four mean-looking soldiers came into the little store. This filled the trio with anything but cheer.

Chapter 6

They were big men, dressed in the same dull pea-green uniforms as all of the others that had invaded their quiet little town. The largest one of them was a redhead. He stood about six foot three, and weighed about 275 pounds. His face was ruddy, almost the shade of his hair. Berets were perched on their heads, and rifles that were beginning to appear commonplace were slung at their sides.

The spokesman of the group took in the room and its occupants with a shrewd glance. He was dark-haired and olive-skinned. He looked as though nothing had ever happened to him that he couldn't handle. He exuded calm and self-control.

"We are installing our computer system in all of your places of business. The bank and credit card system that you use is outdated. Your currency is also soon to become obsolete. Everyone will be given a few months to go to banks, straighten out all of their affairs, and hand in any money that is left in circulation. Then the new system will take over."

He went on. "It's a superior system. All of the old methods are fallible. Cards and money can be stolen or counterfeited. There are many ways of cheating others with the old method. Robberies are committed, causing unnecessary injuries and deaths. Then the perpetrators are locked up and kept at the expense of the entire community, including the persons that have already been defrauded.

"We have a much better way," he went on pompously. "In the future, a scanner will read a microchip that has been implanted in either the hand or the forehead. We are putting the scanners in now. It will take a few months. In the meantime, we are going to start inserting the implants. A microchip will be inserted just under the skin. It won't be much different than the ones that are put into your animals in order to reclaim them if they are lost. The purpose will be different for humans, but very effective also.

"We will be able to keep track of everyone in the world. Think of that. No one will be able to escape justice. In addition, everyone will benefit by just allowing themselves to be scanned at check-out counters like the one we are placing on your counter now. The money will be transferred from account to account instantly. There'll never be a need to carry money or credit cards again.

'When everything has been set up worldwide, no one will buy or sell without the mark that signifies the implant. It isn't painful. Our whole army has already received the implants. There was a slight discomfort for a day or two that wasn't much worse than some inoculations that I've experienced."

Two of the men, the redhead and one of the others, started to work as the other two watched. The unit was installed. The tension mounted with each minute the soldiers lingered. After what seemed like an eternity, the men turned to leave. The one who had been doing all the talking suddenly turned to Chrissie.

"Aren't you usually at the hair salon?" he queried. She got the message and, frightened by the thought that he knew where she should be, scurried out the door.

Jeff was already finished, but reluctant to attract attention to by leaving. Now he knew that it was time to get out of there. As he was heading out the door, one of them called him back. He stood there, not knowing what to expect, and was relieved when the man said.

"Got any chocolate milk in your van?"

They all left together, which left no chance for Dan and Jeff to speak.

Chapter 7

When he was alone, Dan took an orange juice out of the cooler and sat on the stool. He looked around. The little store that his mother and father had opened thirty years ago was still going strong. The magazine rack was full. The newspapers were usually on the bottom shelf. The counter was the length of the shop. One end was reserved for the cash register, and the rest of the green Formica counter was used as the bar of a coffee shop. There were ten matching green leather stools.

Dan sold ice cream, hot dogs, hamburgers, cold drinks, sandwiches, and desserts that he bought from a lady who baked them fresh every morning. She usually brought them in before now. It didn't really matter if she was late today. Most of his regular customers hadn't even come in.

The few groceries that he carried were on shelves at the back end of the store. His parents had started with groceries, but after they died, a big food chain had opened up in town and Dan couldn't compete with their prices. That was when he had remodeled and added a grill and a soda fountain. He carried some candy and magazines. Changing things around had enabled him to stay in business.

Joe hadn't come in, either. Joe was his only employee. He was an elderly man and worked part-time. Dan had hired him because he knew that the stringy, tanned old man needed to earn enough to live on. Joe had come into town one day and had taken a room at the little hotel on the main street, just across from Dan's store. He wandered around the town a bit after that, came into the store one day, and casually asked if Dan knew of anyone that wanted help. Observing him closely as he deliberated his answer, Dan could see that the man's nonchalant demeanor didn't match his hungry eyes, and he decided to take a chance on him.

He had never been sorry. The old man had gradually taken to being quite fatherly to Dan. He also was a perfectionist. Everything that he did was his very best effort. He did the small chores around the shop willingly and well. The customers liked the crusty old guy, too, and business was good enough to keep him on. He was quick-witted and his fast retorts made everyone laugh. He didn't talk much about himself, however, except to say that he was a changed man. It was very unusual for him to be late, and Dan started to worry a little. He could sure use him today, if only to talk to.

Dan was anxious to go home. He wanted to find whatever his mother had left for him in her Bible.

Chapter 8

It was close to noon, and only a few customers had come in. One of them was Rob, the town constable. The area was patrolled daily by the O.P.P. They had an office in town. It was almost always unmanned. Rob's office was operated from a tiny room in the town hall. It was also usually unmanned. Rob, with his prematurely gray hair and shrewd black eyes, was the one who handled most of the police business in town. While there really wasn't a great volume of crime, he still had to be on the road constantly answering the calls that came in. He made good use of an ordinary call answering system and his car phone.

Rob was about six feet two inches, and his hefty frame was mostly muscle. He got few arguments from anyone, except perhaps the odd drunk that was too stupefied to be afraid. He was a good-natured guy who thought that he was lucky to be back here stationed in his home town. He had been in a special service branch before applying for this job. Life was so dull here that he figured on living long enough to retire, instead of getting himself killed like some of the cops he had worked with in Toronto. He knew that he would be backed up by the O.P.P. if there was any serious trouble. This was the closest he had come to needing help, and today, so far, there had been no sign of the two provincial police officers who were regulars on this patrol.

Dan was glad to see him. He had a million questions to ask.

Rob soon disappointed him by saying, "What's going on? It seems like about thirty percent of Wright's Mines is missing. I've been to accident after accident where one of the persons that obviously must have been involved just wasn't anywhere to be found. The fire department is operating shorthanded and isn't even trying to put out the fires. They're just wetting the surrounding buildings.

"I've had hundreds of calls about missing children. The school is totally devoid of kids. The O.P.P. haven't shown up for their regular drive-through patrol. You'd better make me a sandwich or something. I've got to get back out there."

Seeing that Rob didn't know any more than he did, Dan poured out two cups of coffee and started making a roast beef sandwich. He knew that it was one of Rob's favorites. He decided that he was hungry, too, and threw out a few more slices of bread and some of the meat for himself as well. They sat side by side on the stools. Neither of them spoke for a while, as they ruminated on the weird scenes that they had witnessed.

Chapter 9

The streets weren't bustling with normal activity, but they also weren't quiet. One parent after another passed the store. They all had the same worried countenances. A few of them called out their children's names, but most of them were too tired. Some came in and looked quickly around. When they didn't see the object of their search, they backed out and continued their futile hunt. When they saw Rob, a few of them just looked at him, pleading wordlessly. He would shake his head sadly. The sorrow on their faces was heartbreaking. The men fell quiet.

Dan broke the silence first. "I want to go home and check something out. Before Mom died, she sort of talked about this happening. She said that one day the whole world would be united. There would be one church that would encompass all of the earth's religions. Mom said that when this happened that there would be a world government. At this time there would also be a world currency system. If that time ever came, and I was told to get marked so that I could buy and sell, I was to refuse. She asked me to look in her Bible for the answers because she had already marked it out for me. It was only a few days before she died. She was so sick and so insistent that I promised her.

"Her eyes shone as she talked about God calling his people off the earth just before these things happened. I think that she referred to it as the rapture. It seemed to be almost like 'Beam me up, Scottie,' on the old *Star Trek* series. What I want to do now is to read the things that she said she marked out for me in her Bible. I know where it is. It's just where she left it, beside her bed."

Rob listened without interruption as he finished up the last of his sandwich. "It sounds kind of far-fetched to me, but who am I to say that in the light of what's happening around here?"

Chapter 10

Dan wrote on a piece of napkin and surreptitiously slid it in front of Rob. Rob read it and checked out the room with the help of a full mirror that was mounted on the wall opposite his stool. He paid particular attention to the area of the cash register. He carefully considered the shiny new whatever-it-was that the soldiers had installed. At length, he said in a subdued voice, "I don't see anything that is recognizable as a video or listening device. Really, if what they say is true, and if we can't get food or pay for anything without a mark, they don't have to monitor us or fight us, because we will soon die out if we don't comply. I think that they are just watching out for groups of people meeting. If we get together, we might be able to figure out what's going on and try to do something about it. History proves that whenever people unite, they can accomplish anything that they imagine. This is where that old motto 'Divide and Conquer' comes from. Keeping us separate will be their main weapon."

"We definitely have to do something. Jeff suggested that we should meet at the old cave. If we act quickly, we may have a chance to stockpile food, water, medicines, bedding, and clothing. There are lots of provisions right in our own houses, and we'll have to see what we can buy before the system takes over. We'll have to keep ourselves alive and plan some kind of resistance."

A soldier walked by and glanced in as he passed. Rob stood up almost casually and put on his cap. Before he left, he said, "Watch who you talk to, only those you are sure of. Tell them to bring as many provisions as they can carry with them and to stay along the tree line as far as possible."

After Rob left, Dan tried to think. *We may be able to survive in the cave and in the old mine tunnels. It's been years since tours ran in those old silver mines.*

There was certainly nothing else around here to attract tourists. The town council decided that some of the shafts might not be safe. As usual, they didn't want to spend the money either to advertise or to repair the unsafe areas, and so the mines were closed. The majority of our young people had already left home in order to find work. With them went the hope of any growth for this town. The older people just wanted to live out their days in peace on their pensions. Some young families had bought up some of the houses. They sold for much less here than anywhere else. That made up for the disadvantages to some people. It meant the breadwinners had a very long drive to work. Kirkland Lake was the nearest city with some industries, and it's fifty miles away. There isn't much chance of finding a good job in this town unless you're a professional or you own a business.

His reverie was interrupted occasionally as customers came in. He served and commiserated with those who were sorrowing, but said nothing about the plans for the meeting. He only told the ones that he knew well and trusted.

One thing that bothered him was the lack of children. After school, they habitually stopped in and deliberated over his candy counter. He kept one well stocked, even though it really was a nuisance. He got a kick out of watching the little guys press their noses against the glass and hem and haw over their selections. Some of the older kids hung out for a while after school. They livened up the place. He enjoyed getting into their conversations as they spun on his stools drinking milkshakes or sodas.

Today not one came in or even walked by. Those soldiers had everyone scared.

Finally it was time to close the store. He wondered why his helper hadn't shown up and decided to go across to the hotel he stayed at to check on him. Even if the day had been strange, the old man could be sick.

Chapter 11

Timing his departure according to missing the rounds of the soldiers caused him to leave just about the time that he usually did. He angled across the street and down to the hotel. Karina was on duty at the desk. In a small place and small hotel like this with little or no walk-in registrants, she sat and did her sewing or knitting or even shelled peas. Most of her guests were single townspeople like Joe. They kept her little establishment going.

She was a prim and proper lady. There were rumors about her being left at the altar on her wedding day and that she had almost had a nervous breakdown over it. All that was way before his time. He only knew that she was a woman who was as good as her word. Usually she was dressed impeccably. Her normal attire was a long skirt and a crisp blouse with a lacy high collar. This was kept modestly closed with a brooch. She had been good to him when he was a child. Once he had overheard his mother telling her friend that it upset her to see how unhappy Karina was. She said that she had never gotten through to her that she didn't have to carry her burdens alone.

Being just a young boy, he wondered what Karina had to carry that was heavy. He'd thought that if she'd asked him, he would have carried it for her. Even his mother said that he was a fine, strong boy. He smiled now as he recalled the incident.

He noticed how wrinkled and old she was becoming. There was bitterness in her features that momentarily disappeared as she smiled. He knew that the expression had no connection with him, however, and he greeted her fondly. He told her his concerns about Joe, and she told him to go right up. She had presumed that Joe was at work. He was always gone long before she took her place behind the desk.

Dan climbed the narrow stairs to the second floor and to the second room on the left. He knocked. He called out but didn't hear any sounds at all from behind the heavy oak door. He went down and asked Karina if she would let him in with her passkey. In answer she put down her half-full pot of peas, reached up and took a heavy brass key ring from its hook under the darkly varnished compartmented mail slot.

Chapter 12

She followed him up the stairs and opened the door. They looked in to find it empty. The bed had been slept in. His clothes were laid out on the chair neatly, as if they were ready for him to put on for the day. Dan was surprised to see a worn black leather Bible on his bedside table along with his watch and a bit of change. Dan remembered Joe telling him that he was a different man. Now he realized what Joe had meant. Joe was like his mom and the neighbors that were missing.

"What's happened to him? Where could he be?" Karina almost wailed out the words.

Dan felt that they didn't have to be concerned about Joe, but if he wasn't mistaken, everyone that was still here had plenty to worry about.

Dan didn't tell her to come to the meeting. She would never be able to find it or get there. He promised himself to let her know what transpired if he got back safely.

He left for home. The streets were quiet now and creepily empty. He had expected to pass people that he could inform about the plan for the evening, but didn't see anybody.

The town was like a war zone. The streets were still blocked by smashed vehicles. Charred buildings dotted the landscape. The smell of smoke and gas permeated the air. He felt as though he was the last man on earth until a truck carrying more soldiers appeared. The foreign vehicle was traveling very slowly. It stopped when it came to Dan and the driver leaned out and warned, "It's almost curfew. I'd advise you to go home."

That was the only thing on his mind anyway. He had to get his mom's Bible and see what she had marked out for him. He didn't believe what she was saying was important at the time, but he sure did now.

The Bible was right where she had left it. He had asked Laura, the woman that came in once a week to vacuum and dust, not to move his mother's things around. As a result, the room and its contents were clean but virtually undisturbed. He sat on her bed and opened the book. On one of the pages at the back he found a message for him. She had written:

My dear son, I guess you've been driven to read this because of some kind of trauma in your life. My advice now is no different than when I was still with you. I tell you again that everything that you need now or will ever need is to be found in Jesus. I know that you are feeling that you don't understand how Jesus can do anything for you. I invite you to talk to Him, right now, before you even read the scriptures I'm going to list them for you to read. Ask Him to forgive your sins and to come and be everything to you; to lead and to direct you; to give you wisdom into how to follow Him. Now, if why you are into this Bible is because there are strange things happening, like disappearances and accidents, read these verses. After you finish, you'll know what's happening. May the Lord show you what to do. I love you, and I fully expect to see you again.

Dan got on his knees the way that he had often seen his mother do. "If You are really listening, forgive me for my sins, and for never truly believing before. If You are real, come into my heart and be my everything as You have been everything to my mother." Strangely, he felt lighter, and cleaner. Carefully and thoughtfully, he read every scripture that his mother had listed.

Chapter 13

As he left his mother's room an hour later, he heard a familiar sound. The methodical clicking of the huge grandfather clock beat its tic-toc, tic-toc tirelessly through the house. It seemed louder than usual because of the stark stillness in the street. The hour rang out and the big, tense man knew it was almost time to leave for the mine shaft.

In his own room he threw on a black sweat suit. It would probably be too warm now but might keep him from being seen on his way back, presuming that he was going to make it back. It would certainly be very dark.

He growling stomach informed him that something should be done about the hunger that was nagging at him. His insides felt as though they were being nibbled on. Quickly he devoured a couple of peanut butter and jam sandwiches. He followed these with a huge mug full of cold milk. After wiping off the white mustache with the back of his hand, he searched the house for his backpack.

He found it in a corner of the basement and packed it as tightly as possible. The entire contents of the medicine cabinet, a can opener, and all the canned goods from the cupboard were stuffed in.

He wondered who would be there. He had only been able to tell Rob. Chrissie, Rob, and Jeff were the only ones that he was sure would try to get there, as well as anybody that they were able to inform. He wished that he could have contacted them, but the soldiers were too visible for him to even try. The phone at the store had no dial tone, and the phone at home was the same. Someone would probably have been listening in, anyway. He set off from the back door of his old gray brick two-story. The hot afternoon sun was lower in the sky now, but it was still daylight. He peered around carefully, noticing the lush greenery of summer and a few birds flitting back and forth as if nothing was wrong.

Dan set off on his trek, comforted by both the cheerful chirping of the birds and by his failure to see anything threatening. At least there was nothing threatening in his backyard. He felt somewhat sneezy because of the unmistakable odors of burnt things, like charcoal and ash. The gas and oil fumes also lingered on the still air, a reminder of the morning terror. These mingled with the sweet strong scents of the roses from the tall thick king rose bushes that hedged the yard. Such a noxious mixture of scents drifted on the breeze that he was sure he could never forget the smell as long as he lived.

He was keyed up!

Chapter 14

Long ago he and his gang had mapped our routes that allowed them to roam not only all over the town, but gave them access to one of the abandoned mine shafts. They called themselves the Silver Dragons. Their secret club was held in one of the tunnels. It wasn't much of a secret to the children. It was made up of most of the boys in the town and a couple of the girls. The back yards of the silver town, nicknamed because it had grown up around the mines, were for the most part just like his. Large flowering bushes, mature trees and shrubs gave the playing children cover as they pretended to be commandos or cowboys and Indians.

Back alleys, too narrow for motorized traffic, ran behind and paralleled the streets. By these they were able to worm their way through the town and into the woods. Once they reached the woods there was clear sailing almost all the way to the mining property. Excitedly, they eluded the security guard that lazily patrolled the perimeter. He was well-known to them, and they weren't afraid of him. The kids were still not willing to be apprehended, however. Discovery, at the very least, would mean being grounded. Worse than that, the secret hideout would probably be revealed, and all of their fun would come to an end.

Tonight, there was much more at stake. He knew that if he was caught out after curfew, they would shoot to kill. Idly he wondered how much it would hurt to be shot. He dismissed the thought. It was better not to let his thoughts wander.

Hopefully his memories of the once familiar old paths would come back as he went on. Thankfully the town hadn't changed much since he was a child. Even now most of the bushes and hedges that had been used as cover back then were still present. He was glad to notice that they, too, had increased in size. He made his way instinctively, without any problem.

There was no sign of soldiers or any of his friends. He worked his way carefully, even in the protection of the thick forested area. He noticed a heightened awareness of the calls of the birds, the sound of his own footfalls, and the beating of his own heart. The odor wasn't as obnoxious here. Thankfully Dan no longer felt like sneezing.

He had come to the edge of the tree line. The tall grasses weren't nearly as tall as he remembered them. This was the part of the trip that the boys had crawled over in their play commando style. He knew that the shaft that was used as an entrance was just ahead, a few hundred feet across the grassy ridge. Getting down on his knees, he prepared for the final stage of his journey.

After what seemed like hours, but couldn't have been more than fifteen minutes, he approached the shaft entrance. It wasn't even well boarded up. Gingerly he entered. No telling what animals had decided that it would make a good home. Thankfully he found nothing very threatening on his way to the cave. Clinging to the smooth wall he felt for the signal wall, as they used to call it. Sure enough, there it was.

Chapter 15

The abandoned silver mine tunnel opened up into a natural cave. The entrance was completely hidden. If James hadn't fallen at that spot so many years ago, they never would have discovered it. As he fell, he grabbed at the wall and his small hand caught at a loose spot. When he was back on his feet, they felt around and discovered that there was an opening. Several huge rocks had fallen and lay in such a way as to cause an optical illusion. It was possible to weave your way between the layers of rock and the boys did. They were thrilled at the discovery of the cave. It was just as huge and impressive now as it seemed to him when he was a child. From somewhere underground, water filled a hollow and forms a large pool. The water overflowed this natural bowl and disappeared into another crevice in the stone floor.

Dan remembered how sweet and good it used to taste. Unhesitatingly, he went over to the pool, cupped his hands, and scooped up a drink. Thankfully, it was still the same. This wonderful, clean water would enable them to have a fresh water supply if it was necessary.

Dan removed his backpack by pulling it around himself. He noticed that light was coming in from slits in the rocks above. He knew that even though the light could enter, the placement of the layers of rock prevented anyone from seeing down from above. As long as there was no light on within the cave itself, it was completely hidden.

Dan removed his backpack by pulling it around and lowered it to the ground. He looked around and perched on a large rock to rest and wait.

A lean, wiry body wriggled its way through the entrance. A good-looking, brown-haired man carrying full hiking gear appeared. Jeff smiled as he caught sight of Dan sitting on his perch. He had entered cautiously until he saw him. He relaxed slightly at the sight of his pal.

Dan looked affectionately at his best friend. His top lip was partially hidden by a mustache. The bottom lip was well-shaped and full. His deep, golden brown eyes weren't sparkling with mischief as they usually were.

"I've never been so scared in my life." Jeff started, "Our camouflage is still in place after all these years. If I hadn't known to look for the signal wall, I'd never have discovered the entrance."

Dan replied, "Me either. Have you been able to tell anybody?"

"Yea, but just a few. I didn't know who I could trust. Some people that I talked to while I was delivering my milk seemed to go for the idea of the whole world uniting. They don't seem to realize if there is one government, with one self-appointed leader, one religion, and one bank, that our freedom of choice has been severely tampered with. I didn't tell anybody except some of the guys from the old gang. How about you?" asked Jeff.

Dan said thoughtfully, "They told us that war will be done away with, and if the entire world is united, there won't be any poverty. At least not the way there is now in the Third World countries. There also won't be so many prosperous countries, and everything will be equalized. In principal it could work, but of course it won't. Hitler's manifesto sounded good in writing.

As long as any one human is going to be in control, it will end up badly. To quote somebody or other, 'Power corrupts, and absolute power corrupts absolutely.' I read that somewhere. To answer your question, I didn't get to tell anybody but Rob and Nancy. Rob said that he might be late, because he had something that he wanted to do. We'll have to think of a way to get people like Nancy over here. Not too many came into the store today. Even the regulars stayed away."

"I'll tell Laura about it when she comes to clean tomorrow. People are pretty much traumatized," agreed Jeff. "We're afraid to go out, even if they did tell us to go about our regular business. Those soldiers get pretty upset if they see any congregating. The whole town is shook up over the missing people, especially the kids. When I delivered to the doctor's house, he said that he had been prescribing nerve pills over the phone. His office had been swamped. Soldiers had come in and ordered everybody to go home. That's when he started to prescribe over the phone. In the late morning, the phones had suddenly gone dead. It really didn't matter. The drugstore had run out of nonprescription drugs, anyway, and said that they probably wouldn't be able to fill prescriptions either by the end of the day. More than one woman was out wandering around calling for her child. I saw Cindy being roughly treated and ordered to stay off of the streets. I felt like a heel watching from the truck and doing nothing to help her. The whole town is blaming the army, but the army seems to think that we conspired to smuggle the kids out of town."

Dan said, "I have an idea of where everyone is. We don't need to worry about them. We are the ones that have to be concerned. I'll wait till everyone comes before I get into what I have learned.

"This cave is exactly the same as when we had our club meetings here. We'll have to do a little exploring and see if we can find another exit. Maybe we'll have to dig one out. More tunnels must almost intersect with this cave. Rob was going to access the land registry office and get the mining maps. He's going to try to destroy all trace of the records of the silver mine tunnel system at the same time. I hope that he can pull it off. The army will certainly know about the mines, but they won't know how easily we get from one seeming dead-end into the next tunnel or cave. I think that you have to be a kid to discover the openings, like we did when we were young." A slight sound caused him to whisper, "Quiet! Listen!"

Chapter 16

Some loose dirt fell down one of the crevices in the ceiling above them. There was a light play as well. A group of soldiers were walking on the rock table over their heads! The two men sat motionless and terrified. Snatches of conversation floated down to them.

"There isn't anything here. Tomorrow we're supposed to search the tunnels."

"I wish we could get back to headquarters for supper."

" Yes, I'm hungry, and I'm sick of walking!"

"The big shots get to travel in style. Do you think they're planning to make us walk all over the whole world?'

"Quit your complaining. You'll be doing worse than that if anyone hears you. Let's join the others. Nothing seems out of place here."

Dan and Jeff stayed very still. They both looked intently and listened with their heads cocked to catch any slight sound until the dust quit falling. They waited until there were no noises at all.

"If they are going to search tomorrow, we'll find out if this is a safe place to use for a headquarters," commented Jeff. "Tomorrow will be the big test."

He was suddenly interrupted. They heard the sound of footsteps. The beam of a flashlight shone out from between the rocks that concealed the tunnel.

Chapter 17

Before the men could scramble out of sight, Rob appeared. His face was red, and he was panting. He turned off his flashlight when he saw them. Rob spoke breathlessly, "I would have been here sooner, but I had to hide in the woods for a while. There was a whole bunch of soldiers snooping around."

"Yea, a few minutes ago they were directly overhead," said Jeff.

"I finally got into the registry office," said Rob. "It took awhile, but Gus got into the computer, copied the records out for us, and erased them. We think we got all of the copies of everything pertaining to the mine from the file room. By the way, Gus is supposed to be here."

"So is Chrissie." said Dan. "I'm a little worried about her. I thought she'd be here by now."

"Have you seen her since this morning?" asked Jeff.

"Yes," replied Dan. "I talked to her for a minute. She was just closing up when I walked by. Some of the army personnel marched by her salon. One of them gave her an appraising look when they saw her talking to me. That was all she needed. She took off immediately towards home. She managed to let me know that she had only told a few of the women that had been part of our gang. She had met or passed them on the street. No one even came in to get a hairdo today."

"Who cared how they looked today?" said Rob.

"We'd better get out of this cave and have a look at the hill the soldiers just walked across. We're going to have to disguise the crevasses with moss or something in case light shows through from the inside."

"Yea," said Jeff, "we'll probably have another hour of daylight."

Dan got onto his feet. "Anybody that doesn't show up by dark probably won't be able to come tonight. It's going to be mainly up to us to make this a temporary shelter until we can devise a safe hiding place. The maps and charts should help us to find intersecting tunnels."

"We've got a big job ahead," said Jeff. "Thank God our old water supply is still trickling in." He walked over to the pool and scooped up a drink. "It's as sweet as I remembered."

"We'll need all of the supplies that we can carry here," Dan mused. "We'll need food, blankets and medicine. It's going to take quite a few trips. If this cave is discovered during the search, they'll just think it's a natural phenomenon that no one knows about. Once they've searched, we should be safe here. Let's get up top and see what we can do about stuffing the cracks in the rocks."

"Let's stash the stuff we brought before we go," suggested Dan.

The three men stuffed the contents of their knapsacks in some recesses. When they finished, they rolled loose rocks around the items, carefully inspected things and were finally satisfied with the result.

Rob pronounced the job, "Great! Completely hidden. We'll have to go back and follow our normal routines for a few days. Every night we'll come back with all that we can carry. If we study the maps, surely we'll find ways to get ourselves around underground."

It won't be easy to get them here, but we need tools, too," said Jeff.

"I think that I can get close enough with my squad car to drop off some shovels in the woods. I'll keep my eyes open and watch for army activity going away from town. They'll have to leave sometime to conduct searches. When they come back, I'll know it's safe for me to leave with all of the tools that I can manage to hide."

"They are still allowing me go on calls," Rob told them. "They informed me that they were in charge. They said that I can go about my regular duties but I have to answer to them now. There weren't any calls after the phones were cut off, but no one stopped me from driving around. There was so much panic, I was flagged down all the time. The worst part was that I didn't know any more than anybody else."

"If you can drop off the tools, try and put them down between the two double birches," said Dan. "You know where I mean. Remember the pit we dug to trap the prince's men? It was directly opposite the oak. It's the same tree that we climbed to pretend we were Robin and his Merry Men. I noticed it when I was on the way here. They'll be safe there. You can get them on your way here tomorrow night."

Chapter 18

I don't know how all this will end, and I'm certainly afraid," Jeff admitted. "One thing I do know. We are going to have to organize, learn how to survive, fight, and resist with every means we can muster up. I don't want to be an unthinking, brainwashed zombie of the New World Order. I'd rather be dead."

"We'll meet here again the night after next. I'd like to do a little exploring before then. There's an old house on the other side of the forest. I'd like to check it out. After they put the highway through, the old road was abandoned. The house was sort of left sitting in the middle of nowhere. There is a lot of vacant land around it. I wonder if it could be of use to us," said Dan. "Why don't you two meet here tomorrow with anyone that shows up? Be careful who you tell. Find out how they feel first," he added, "and make sure that they know to bring all of the nonperishables or medicines that they have at home. We don't know when we will need it in order to survive."

The men left together, but as soon as they reached the mouth of the tunnel, they allowed five minutes between themselves. Dan was the last to leave, and the trip home was as uneventful as the trip to the mine.

The next evening, Dan prepared himself for an adventure. He couldn't remember ever feeling so alive. He had seen Chrissie and found out that she had been afraid to leave her house. She had gotten some goods together and dressed herself in dark clothes. She checked out of her windows and found that soldiers were walking around on patrol. She thought it was best to stay in.

Chapter 19

Roaring and sputtering jarred the quiet. Curious, Jo-Anne went outside. They smirked at the diminutive, apple-doll-like creature from their jeeps. They laughed when she stuck out her chin bravely and asked what they wanted.

"Are you alone here?" one of the soldiers demanded.

"Yes," she answered.

"We are going to search your house. I suggest that you sit over there until we're through." He indicated an old wicker rocking chair that was sitting on the porch. She wisely obeyed.

Surprisingly, after what seemed like a long time to her, they left her to her rambling home. She overheard them asking what should be done with her. After a bit of deliberation that she couldn't quite hear, she was ordered to stay put until someone came and got her to be marked. She didn't know what they were talking about. They obviously thought that she wasn't capable of understanding because they didn't offer to explain. Jo-Anne thought that it would be prudent to allow them to think of her that way. It could be useful to her later.

Jo-Anne's vantage point afforded a panoramic view. She had climbed the stairs to the third floor and was watching the departure of the army jeeps and the men that had been on foot. A flash of movement in the field caught her attention. A man was crawling toward her house, unaware of the men that had just left her property. She knew that they would still be able to spot him if any of them turned a head.

As she was thinking that, it happened! One of them stumbled, and when he looked back to see what had tripped him, he also saw the dark figure that was creeping through the tall grass. The creeper was angling toward the edge of the field. Suddenly he saw the soldiers that were filing away from him. He froze, but the one who had caught sight of him turned and came back.

As he was turning, he yelled, "I think there's something going on back there! Permission to investigate?"

"Take two men with you."

"Vandermyer! Collins! Come with me!"

In the time that it took for them to organize themselves, Dan, for he was the man that had been crawling, jumped to his feet like an athlete, made a run for the house, entered, and closed the door behind him.

Jo-Anne had seen the whole thing from behind her lacy curtains. She was there facing him as he entered. "Follow me!" she ordered.

He followed her as closely as possible. At first he could hardly believe what was happening. She had beckoned him in. They had gone straight into the warm library of the big old house. The afternoon sun had made the large room seem almost cozy. The tiny wizened creature that was ahead of him seemed unreal.

Over her shoulders he could see a massive fireplace. It was large enough for a man to stand in. A faint scent of mustiness came from an extensive book collection. The shelves that flanked the fireplace were full of them. Straw and horsehair stuffing in the well-worn satin chairs lent their own peculiar odor. The walls of this room were covered in heavy red brocade. His eyes took in the scene without conscious thought. Obediently he stepped after her.

Suddenly something she did startled him to full attention.

She reached out a hand that reminded him of a monkey's claw. He had seen one once in a market in Korea. Her fingers touched something and the entire bookcase to the left of the fireplace swung creakily open. A wide passageway, dark and dank, was exposed. She noticed his apprehension and smiled at him. Her almost toothless smile did nothing to relieve his anxiety. Dan felt as though he had been transported into an old horror movie. She took a flashlight from the frilly white apron that she wore over her severe black dress. She reminded him of a very decrepit French maid, and he smiled to himself.

    He could see now that they were in a very well-constructed tunnel. It wasn't as large as the mine tunnel but appeared to be solid. As they went, she told him the story. Her father and his father before him were mobsters. This house was built during Prohibition.

Chapter 20

She led him through the passage that seemed to have a lot of twists and turns. She explained that since the work had been done surreptitiously, they hadn't blasted through rock, but patiently dug around it.

Finally they came up to a set of stairs. The tunnel went on, but she stopped there. She asked him to go up first, because there was a heavy door that had to be pushed up. Her ancient frame was not strong enough to lift it. She hadn't had any reason to use the tunnel for years.

It took a bit of strength, but the thought of the soldiers that most certainly would be on his heels gave him the extra adrenaline that he needed. She disappeared into the opening and he followed quickly. The door was lowered, and they stood motionless, listening. They were in the woods. Thickets and briers hid them from view, but they heard the soldiers' comments that were being carried on the wind.

"I know that I saw him go into that old house, but he's not there now."

"We would have seen him come out. I think that you're imagining things, as usual." There was some general laughter, and the voices trailed away as the men moved off.

"They're gone," she cackled. "This is the most fun I've had in years."

"What kind of house is this?" asked Dan, who was still confused about everything. "What's this tunnel that we've just used?"

"This place was a gambling joint and speakeasy during Prohibition, and afterwards, because of its reputation, people from all over the country came here." She went on proudly to give him the history of the two-hundred-year-old house. One of its most popular features was the passageway that could be accessed from several rooms. No one was ever arrested while they were here, although there had been a few raids. Thanks to her father's ingenuity, they had made a fortune. Most of their clientele had been prominent citizens who, while they could well afford the expensive diversion, couldn't afford to get caught. This safety feature combined with the opulence of the huge house, made it a very popular spot.

"Where does the tunnel end?" Dan questioned.

"They actually broke into the mine shaft and had to backtrack. I remember that they had quite a time trying to repair the hole they made as they broke into that silver mine. Lucky for them the miners were on strike right then.

"When Daddy died, he left this place to my brother and me. My brother died about ten years ago. Before he died, he stocked the bunker with food and water. For a few years, all people talked about was being prepared for a nuclear attack. I don't know what's here, but I know that nothing has been touched for many years, and everything was put here that was necessary for survival.

"My brother wouldn't carry on with Daddy's business," she reminisced. "I really wanted him to, but he said that the Lord would provide money for us some other way. He was always talking about the Lord. He even got my son to be the same as him.

"The both of them kept at me, but I just ignored them. If my husband hadn't died, he would have convinced them that it was silly to waste this set-up. Imagine them just running this place like any ordinary hobby farm."

Dan felt hope rising. Maybe they could survive using these tunnels. If they could get to their cave from the tunnel system, they would be able to organize themselves.

Chapter 21

The old girl was certainly all right upstairs. Her memory was fantastic.

"How have you been living way out here? You seem to be pretty isolated."

"Yes," she answered, "it wasn't always like this. The old highway went right past. There were other farms around."

"What happened to them?"

"The owners died off, the county moved the main road, and here we sit in the middle of nowhere."

"You seem to be alone. How do you manage?"

"Oh, I haven't been alone. My son still lives here on the weekends. We do a little farming. There's a cow and a goat. We also have a few chickens and ducks. My son, Derek is his name, travels into the city and stays there all week. He has a good job working for an insurance company. He was supposed to come home yesterday, but he didn't show up. He's never done this before, and I'm worried about him. There's been such a hullabaloo. I've never heard the like. It sounded like bombs going off, sirens, and soldiers! I've never seen anything as strange as this in all of my life, and I'm ninety-three now."

Dan told her what had happened in town. He described what he had seen himself, and what he heard from his friends. He explained that his mother also talked about the Lord, just the way her brother and her son had. Lastly, he explained the passages of scripture from Thessalonians and Revelation that he hadn't believed a few short days ago. He told her that one day there was to be a catching up to heaven of everyone who trusted in the Lord Jesus Christ as their Savior.

Jo-Anne broke in with, "Yes, that's the way George and Derek always talked. That's what they always said to me. I said that if I was as good as I could be then I was going to heaven, but they said that wasn't true, and I always got mad and walked away."

"Well, I know that I felt that way, too, but now all of the children are missing. Everyone that used to talk like that seems to be gone, too. I went into a fellow's room to look for him. His name was Joe, and he did a little work for me. He never did say much, but I found a Bible beside his bed, just like my mother always had beside her bed. My mom's friends weren't in their house, but the coffee was on, and there were signs that they had been in the middle of breakfast."

He went on thoughtfully, "Something strange happened to me when I read the Bible. I did believe, and I did what my mother wanted me to do. I thought very hard about my life and realized that even though I'm not as bad as some other people that I know, as far as God is concerned, sin is sin. There were many things that I had to ask Him to forgive me for. Then I thought about all the people who had done things to hurt me, and I knew that I had to forgive them. When I was finished talking to God, I felt clean inside. Now I know that when I die, I really will meet my mother in heaven. Jo-Anne, would you like to feel clean inside, too?"

She hung her head; there was a tear at the corner of one of her eyes. "Yes," she said, "I want to know that when I die I can go to heaven. I really do. Do you think that my son Derek has disappeared from off this earth, and he's in heaven right now?"

"I don't know," Dan said honestly.

Dan showed her the scriptures that his mother had marked out for him. He had copied them onto a sheet of paper and had carried it folded in his pocket ever since. He had read the words so often over the last few days that he was almost able to recite the different verses. He shared them with her now, and at the end of it he prayed with her, and she asked Jesus to come into her heart and cleanse her from every sin. Her face was alight with something that hadn't been there before, and Dan knew that she was feeling the way he had. He was filled with pleasure at the sight of her old wrinkled face.

Chapter 22

Dan told her about the cave and the other people who were going to refuse to be marked. "We need to become organized and hide from the army until we can figure out how to survive and how to convince others not to take the mark. We have only a few weeks to get prepared. They are setting up all over the world. Their plan is being implemented already, but there must be others that don't want this to happen. We have to try to network. We need to have a safe place to work from, and live in, until we figure out how to live without buying or selling. Living without money seems impossible. The alternative is allowing ourselves to be marked, and God warns us not to."

Jo-Anne interjected, "We can see what supplies are still in the tunnel. You can use my house at one end and the entire tunnel system. It won't be too hard to break through at the end again and that will hook us up to the mine shaft and all of its tunnels and caves."

"We can sneak into town from the cave. There's a route that we used as kids," Dan said with excitement. "They won't be too worried about finding us because they will expect us to just die out from hunger or thirst or the need of medicine."

The woman listened as carefully as she could. She felt that she was receiving too much information too quickly.

"The faster we get supplies stocked up, the better," Dan was saying. "I'll have to go back now. Tomorrow I'll go to work at the store and let the gang know to work at stocking the cave. Later we'll try and knock the wall down and find some way to disguise the hole."

Dan offered to accompany her back to the house, but she refused.

"I'm quite able to get myself around," she said testily. "I've been doing it for 90 years now." The door was lifted, and the feisty old lady disappeared down the steps. He was lowering the door after her when he thought of Karina.

"If I brought a lady to your house, would you sort of look after her until we get established?" he asked.

"Sure, I could use the company. I haven't had a woman to talk to for a long time," she replied. "The last female visitor I had here was a girl that Derek was interested in. Nice girl, her name was Ashley. He met her just before he got a big promotion. She was working in the office that they sent him to. He wanted to marry her, but he wasn't sure if he should. I know that he was in love with her, but he wanted a woman that would love God as much as he did. I told him that he was crazy not to snatch her up, but he said he'd rather be safe than sorry."

Dan patiently listened to her rambling, and said, "This lady isn't young. Her name is Karina. She owns the hotel in town. I'll try to convince her to come with me on my next trip here." He added, "I feel that it's time I left."

"I hate to see you go," said Jo-Anne sincerely.

"Don't worry, you'll be hearing from me soon. Is there anything that you are in need of? I can bring it to you when I return. Don't be surprised if I have a few people with me. We'll involve you in our plans, and we'll need to use your house as well as the tunnels and mine shafts. This storeroom is wonderful. We'll be able to use it as a center. It just could enable us to survive."

She shook her head. "I'm fine right now," she said.

He came close to her and gave her a hug. She grinned happily, showing a partial row of brownish-yellow teeth that no longer stood straight as they once had. At her age, it was a wonder that she had any teeth. She waved as he lowered the heavy door. He checked around before he took off sprinting back through the woods toward the town.

Chapter 23

"We'll meet at the lookout one month from today at sunset," Derek promised her. "By that time we should know what we want to do about us." He was doubtful that a marriage between them could work. Divorce was definitely out as far as he was concerned. It was imperative that he be certain. The commitment would be for the rest of their lives.

Ashley knew that they would be happy. A month was far too long to go without seeing him. She loved him so much that she herself, by sheer willpower, would make their marriage a success. She remembered the day that she had taken a seat beside him in the cafeteria. It had certainly caused a buzz of gossip when she sat down at his table. Their co-workers soon got used to the fact that they were an item. She and Derek had discovered that their paths had almost crossed before. In fact, he lived on a farm about five miles away from a mining town where her father had worked. She went over those first conversations with pleasure. It seemed as though she could remember how he looked as he talked to her. She noticed that he always held her eyes as he talked. This was unusual in a man. It gave her the opinion that he was honest and straightforward.

Chapter 24

Several days before the time specified, Ashley drove to the area of the lookout. She had taken some vacation time and booked a room in a nearby motel.

She was happy with her choice. It was a neat little house. The front room had been converted into an office. A row of rooms had been added on later, one at a time, she suspected, as the owners prospered. The young woman got out of her car, stretched, and went on into the office. It smelled a lot like fresh bread was baking somewhere at the back of the house. A little china bell sat on a shiny mahogany desk that must have come from an auction sale. It looked like an antique that had once graced a fancy hotel. Ashley rang the bell, and a few minutes later a small plump lady came out, wiping floury hands on her apron as she approached.

"You must be Miss Keean," she said with a pleasant smile. "Welcome, your room is ready for you. Did you bring provisions?" she added. "You know that it's a housekeeping room, but perhaps you don't know that the town is about ten miles away." Without giving Ashley a chance to answer, she went on. "If you didn't bring food with you, we can arrange to provide you with two good meals a day. You can just come and eat with me and my husband in our kitchen."

When she stopped for a breath, Ashley said, "No, thank you. I've brought everything that I need and I really want to be alone. I'd like to take walks and rest. Could I see the room now?" As the pair walked to the designated room, Ashley sniffed the fresh air.

There were heady scents she recognized. They emanated from the carnations and petunias that bordered the many well-tended beds of shrubbery and flowers that were planted around the house. Bricked paths meandered aimlessly. One ended at a small bench. Another led into a wilderness path. Ashley decided to explore a little during her stay. Deb, for that was how she introduced herself, kept up a steady chatter. *She is probably a bit lonely out here,* thought Ashley. When the mine closed, a lot of other businesses had suffered, including this one. She seemed to be the only guest.

Deb led the way in, still chattering. Now the woman was talking about God.

Was she the only person in the world that didn't care about God? That is, if He even existed. Everyone she met lately acted like they actually knew Him. As far as Ashley was concerned, God was the only problem between her and Derek. She looked around the neat little room when she entered, taking the whole thing in at a glance.

A double bed, desk, and dresser were on one side. There was a small television with rabbit ears, of all things, on the other side of the room. There was a door leading to the bathroom, a small drop-leaf table with two chairs, a range, and a small refrigerator. The bathroom boasted a window with a view of forest greenery that cheered Ashley up somewhat.

It was not much different from those that most other motels offered. She was weary from the long drive. When the door closed after Deb left, she set about unloading the few groceries that she had brought, hung up her clothes and headed for the bathroom for a long soak. Finally she fell into a fitful sleep that left her still tired the next morning.

With all of the exercise that she got on her walk the next day, she expected to sleep well, but the bed creaked and complained as she turned all night long. She remembered that she once had motion sickness pills in a little pillbox in her purse. She checked and found some. They usually put her to sleep. She took two that evening.

There were very limited television stations available with the rabbit ears, and she had finished the book that she brought. The only reading material that was to be found was a Gideon Bible. She perused it casually and was interested in the names of former readers that were recorded inside the cover page. Suddenly the lights went out. She was becoming very sleepy. *So what if it's dark,* she thought, she was in bed anyway. Lazily she thought of how she'd met Derek.

Chapter 25

The lineup was long, as always. Ashley carefully looked over the sandwiches. Her favorite fillings were always tucked inside the wrong type of bread. Her choice would have been an egg salad on brown. Resignedly, she picked up a plain cheese on white. Desserts were plentiful, mouth-watering, and varied. She picked up a baked custard because all of the more delectable desserts were just too fattening.

Carrying her tray expertly, she made her way across the crowded cafeteria. There was an empty seat next to Derek Foster. She longed to sit with him. He was new. She wanted to get to know him. The table that she usually occupied was peopled with a few of the girls in her department and a couple of salesmen. If she sat with Derek, the gossip would be outrageous. Rumors spread quickly through the offices of the Benson Insurance Company.

Ashley smiled at Derek, who was looking up at her, but she walked resolutely past his table to take up her usual place.

She set down her tray, pulled out her chair, and sat down to eat and catch up to the conversation. Cynthia was saying, "I hear that he's been groomed to take Mr. Arthur's place."

Ashley knew the subject of the day would be speculation about Derek.

"I found out that he's single. He lives with his mother," offered Ian triumphantly.

"Ben said that he likes to skydive," Ali interjected. "Apparently, he's a weekend farmer, and he spends his vacations rock climbing or hiking."

Derek had arrived just last week. He was a top salesman who had worked his way up through the ranks. The vice president of the company was retiring. Several of the highest ranking salespeople were after his job. There was a lot of backbiting and jealousy between the hopefuls. Ashley knew what she was listening to was idle gossip with a few sour grapes.

When lunch was over, the group headed back to the office. As she walked by the sales office, John stuck his head out of his doorway. "Hi," he said, "are you game for supper at six at La Pollo?"

"Okay with me." Ashley smiled and went on quickly toward her office. She had gone out to dinner a few times with him, but so far no bells or whistles.

Until now only one man had affected her like that. His name was Jeff. He had been a bright and upcoming salesman. His career had taken over his whole life. One evening he phoned her. "I'm going back home!" he said. "Life shouldn't be a rat race. The town I grew up in is peaceful. You can enjoy life there, and you don't have to impress anyone. I'm sure that I'll miss you, though. If you ever come to Wright's Mines, I'll be there."

She had been sorry, too. She had once lived near Wright's Mines. It was a small town, with few jobs, and some unhappy memories. She had to earn a living, and her job held promises of promotions. She couldn't just follow him. After all, he hadn't really proposed. She never even had a chance to find out how he felt about her. She sighed. When was she going to do something gutsy? It seemed like she always took the safe route.

Chapter 26

She shook herself from her reverie. The day went like a flash. She was aware that it was time to go home when she heard her coworkers teasing her.

"Are you that ambitious?" asked Tasha.

"Knock it off!" Tonya joked.

"Old man Henry isn't here to watch you do your eager beaver act," added Laurie.

She finished up. As she left the almost empty building, she literally bumped into Derek Foster. As he broke her fall, Ashley noticed that his deep brown eyes had little golden flecks. She also saw the concerned look on his face as he held her until she was steady.

"I'm sorry," he said. "You're Ashley, aren't you?" He spoke in the most resonant voice that she had ever heard.

"Ashley Keean," she replied. *It was no wonder that he was a top salesman*, she thought. *Not many would be able to resist a sales pitch made with that voice.*

"Could we go somewhere for coffee?" he asked.

She knew that she was to meet John at six. If she had a coffee now, she wouldn't have time to change for her date. She didn't deliberate long. "All right."

They went to a nearby donut shop. He wasn't just a good

speaker. He knew how to listen as well. Soon she surprised herself by telling him small details of her life that she considered intimate. He was charming and open. Sometimes they interrupted each other. They would both laugh and apologize profusely.

She was enchanted. He seemed to be everything that she had ever wanted. She liked his attitude on life and the people around him. They were on the same wavelength. They enjoyed the same things, and she was totally easy in his presence.

Too quickly she noticed that it was almost six. She would have to get moving to make it to the restaurant.

She and Derek said their goodbyes on the sidewalk in front of the coffee shop. She declined his offer of a ride home, and without argument, he flagged down a cab for her.

John had been waiting, but not patiently. She could see by the look on his face that he was surprised to see her dressed as she had been all day at work.

He peevishly began speaking as soon as she was seated. "You're ten minutes late. I'm so hungry that I've already ordered. I asked for paella for you because I remember you had it the last time."

Yes, she thought to herself. *I did eat that last time, but only because you keep ordering what you want for me.*

He had opted to sit in an intimate corner. She preferred to sit where she could watch the traffic and life itself pass before her through the plate glass window. She had mentioned that many times, but he didn't remember the things that she told him.

She realized that they didn't really communicate. He gossiped about other people in his office and confided how much he wanted this promotion. His criticisms bothered her. He went on vehemently. According to John, he was the only one that deserved the job. Everyone else was inept.

Ashley found herself thinking about Derek and their flowing conversation. Had John always been like this? Why hadn't she noticed? The long dinner over, she was grateful when he dropped her off at the subway.

The ride home gave her time to think. Would she always not make waves? Would she always do what was expected, eat what she didn't really like, and choose ordinary custard to finish her meal? Would she always sit and listen to conversations that annoyed her? Was she ever going to begin to live?

The next day, she stood before the counter in the cafeteria. *Amazing*, she thought. There's one egg salad sandwich on brown bread. A row of strawberry shortcakes were right beside the custards. The berries were plump and whipped cream rose to little peaks on top. She chose the nicest one. Carrying her tray took concentration. She was frowning slightly as she neared the table where Derek was already seated. She looked up to see him smiling at her.

"Won't you join me?" he said.

She did, without even the slightest hesitation.

Chapter 27

As she drifted off to sleep, she was still thinking about Derek. She had finally decided to take a risk and look at what was happening. Would he want to marry her? Would he even show up to tell her if he'd decided to call it quits with her? Suddenly she had a desire to pray, but she didn't know how. She said out loud, "God, if You are real, and I'm not sure that You are, I want You to show me. I really want to marry Derek. Please help me to know You like he does so that he'll marry me."

She slept like she was dead for fifteen hours. Her surprise of finding that it was afternoon was followed by a wonderful feeling of well-being. She was famished, and prepared herself a breakfast of instant porridge, tea, and a banana.

A desire to actually read the Bible that was on the night table came over her. She started at the beginning. The next couple of days went quickly, until the day that she was to meet Derek. Finally, she packed up, including the Bible that wasn't hers, and looked around at the little room that had been her home for the last few days. She felt that she was leaving a bit of herself behind. Ashley always had this notion as she vacated spaces that she didn't expect to revisit. A tiny feeling of loss washed over her.

It seemed like the clock was hardly moving as she waited to leave. She expected to pay with her credit card on leaving, but no one was around. The office door was open, and after calling for a few minutes with no results, she returned to her room. She took what she thought she owed in cash and left it on the dresser. She wrote a note offering to pay for the book and anything else that she might owe them if they'd bill her.

The road stretched out before her. It was strangely empty. There wasn't any sign of life as she drove to the deserted lookout area just before sunset. It didn't bother her that it was such a lonely area. Since the mines had closed, there probably hadn't been many tourists. She parked in the empty space that used to be a well-cared-for lot. Grass and weeds had broken through the asphalt and parts had heaved up causing deep cracks and dips. Derek wasn't there. Her heart sank. Ashley was sure now that he wouldn't come.

This hadn't been anticipated. He was so very dependable and if he wasn't going to marry her she expected that he would have told her in person. She climbed up the steep steps to the top of the wooden structure. Rough wooden chairs had been placed there long ago. They stood in two rows, overlooking the rolling hills that cradled a picturesque lake. The forest provided the background, but she totally missed the beauty of the scene. As the sun slowly set, Ashley didn't notice the radiant pinks, purples or reds of the sunset. She didn't notice the softness of the breeze that carried the scents of pine, and the wildflowers that covered the hills. Her eyes filled with tears, and she sobbed out the pain in her heart. Maybe she didn't love God, but no one would ever love Derek more than she did.

Chapter 28

Dan had been exploring as he made his way back. He was approaching the lookout when he became aware of heartrending sobs. The sounds whirled down to him from above by way of the breeze. It was almost dark, but he could make out the slender figure of a woman. She was on the top deck and as he neared her, she became aware of his shadowy presence.

"Derek!" she cried down to him. "You did come."

"I'm sorry," Dan called up to her, "but I'm not whoever you were expecting. Can I do anything to help you? You seem to be in distress." He stood right below her.

Ashley had been surprised out of her weeping, and although she wanted to be alone, she answered him.

"No, there's nothing that anyone can do." For some reason that she didn't understand, she told him, "Someone was supposed to meet me here tonight at sunset. It was very important to me."

"I don't think that you should be out here. Maybe whoever was supposed to meet you has been prevented by curfew. You could be shot if anyone sees you out after dark. I've never seen you before. You aren't from around here."

"No, but I lived here for a little while when I was young. My dad was a miner. We lived in the miners' shacks that were west of town. He was killed, and my mom took us to the city. I've only been back once, just a few weeks ago. My boyfriend wanted me to meet his mother. She lives somewhere around this area. I hadn't even realized that she lived near Wrights Mines."

"Her name wouldn't be Jo-Anne, would it?" Dan asked with some surprise.

"Why, yes, Jo-Anne Foster. She lives in a wonderful old house that used to be a speakeasy. Do you know Derek's mother?" Ashley spoke out quickly in her excitement. Then she added hopefully, even before he could answer, "Do you really think that Derek was unable to get here? What could have stopped him?" Then she added, as if it just struck her, "What do you mean, curfew?"

"Don't you know what's happened around here?" asked the flabbergasted man. "There is a curfew now. No one is allowed to be out after dark! There's been an invasion. There have been sirens and blasts that shook everything around! An army marched into town! Hundreds of people are missing, not to mention every single person under the age of twenty. In answer to your question, yes, I think that Derek either disappeared with all of the others or he's been prevented from coming to meet you."

"Disappeared!" the frightened woman burst out. "Please tell me! What's going on?"

"How could you not know? There's been so much noise and confusion!" Dan was incredulous.

"I've been alone. I hadn't slept for a few nights. I was so tired that I conked out for about fifteen hours. I did have a dream that seemed real, though. I heard a lot of noise and had a dream about being in London during the bombings. I dreamed that I was a schoolgirl. I was forced to dive into the ditch on my way to school. I woke up feeling wonderful after having all of that sleep and spent the next few days just reading, thinking, and believe it or not, praying. When I left the motel that I was staying at, the owners were nowhere around. I had to leave what I thought I owed them. They have my name and address in case it wasn't enough."

Chapter 29

"You'd better come with me." Dan looked up at the sky. "It's almost dark already. Have you any other clothes with you? You won't be able to walk far in those." He pointed at her high heels.

"Yes, I have some runners in the car. I'll get them." She got a jogging outfit as well as the runners and put it on over her clothes. He was pleased to see how quickly she got ready to go with him.

He led the way back to the old house. She kept up well. It wasn't too far away.

"Where are we going?" Ashley asked.

"I think that you'll be surprised to see where we end up."

He was sure by now that she was the girl that Jo-Anne had mentioned. He hadn't had a chance to answer her question earlier. He decided to wait and see if he was right.

There wasn't anything to hinder them. He guessed that the patrol was back in town by now and would be checking the streets for any curfew breakers.

It was quite dark when they reached the farmhouse. The full moon greatly helped him to get his bearings, and they made their way up onto the porch. The house was almost dark. When they knocked on the door, a sliver of light appeared. He guessed that Jo-Anne had been in the library.

Her shadowy little figure appeared, and she peered out from behind her lacy curtains. The wrinkled face was tense until Dan said, "It's okay, Jo-Anne. It's me, Dan. I've brought someone with me."

She broke into a grin then, revealing her snaggletooth smile, and opened the door to admit them. She and Ashley recognized each other and hugged.

"Where's Derek?" the old lady questioned anxiously. "Have you seen him? Is he alright?" She asked the questions so fast that Ashley didn't get time to answer. When she finally could, she said, "I'm so sorry, but I don't know. He was supposed to meet me, and he didn't."

"I have an idea where he is then. I'll tell you all about it later. Come on in."

Chapter 30

Dan used the tunnel to return home. He emerged in the woods, had to circumvent the mines, and then he took the old trails back into his yard.

It was quite dark. He would be late, but he was still going back out in a while to meet the others.

He entered his house without incident, and breathed a sigh of relief. In a day or so he would be living in the headquarters. There was a lot to be done until then.

A small sound coming from the front room alerted him to the fact that he might not be alone. Cautiously he listened. Not hearing anything further, he took off the hiking boots that constrained his feet. He wasn't used to long walks. His feet ached even more when he removed them as the blood started to flow properly again. He put on the kettle. It had been a long time since lunch. He was heading over to the fridge when he heard the noise again. This time he was sure that he heard something. He went into the dining room, and turned on the light.

Chrissie appeared in the doorway between the dining room and the front room. His heart had been thumping and when she appeared, it did nothing to calm him down. It took a minute for him to realize who she was.

"I'm sorry for scaring you, Dan." Her eyes were big, and he

knew that she had been frightened as well. All this business of sneaking around was getting to her, too.

He went over to her and hugged her. "I'm so glad that you're all right. I've been worried about you ever since you left the store the other day." He'd hugged her before, of course, occasions like his mother's funeral; again, at her wedding; and when her brother had been involved in an accident. Once again, it was hard to let her go. *When this is over,* he vowed to himself, *I'm going to ask her to marry me.*

" Jagger has been keeping in touch with Jeff. He told me what's been going on," Chrissie told him. "I tried to get to the cave once. Just before I was ready to leave, I saw that there were soldiers hanging around and I couldn't go out in case they followed me."

Jagger was one of her brothers; he was totally reliable, and Dan was glad that he was with them. He would be a great help. He was strong, and had been in the army for a while. He wouldn't have any trouble going back and forth between the town and the cave.

"Where is he now?" asked Dan. He felt that it was time that they got together in a group to discuss their plans.

"He's gone to the cave with some groceries. We've been raiding the houses of the people that have disappeared. We've been taking all that we can carry to the cave. Rob has left several loads at the drop-off spot. After dark we have been carting the supplies the rest of the way."

"How many people do we have now who know about this?" asked Dan.

Chrissie answered, "I'm sorry to say that there are only about thirty besides us." She continued, "Everyone else seems to be quite taken with the idea of a world government. They think it will be like Shangri-La. They expect life to be the closest thing to perfect that we've ever dreamed of."

"I was concerned about that happening." Dan had expected that from the beginning. "Are they still meeting tonight? I closed the store and went away before dark. There were some customers, but I didn't see anybody I knew that I could trust all day."

"Yes." she said, "I've been waiting for you, and I didn't want to start out by myself."

He announced proudly, "I've made some discoveries that will make our plans possible."

He told her about Jo-Anne, the house, the tunnels, and the storeroom. She was amazed that something like that was under their noses all these years and they never had discovered it.

"Let's go!" he said. "It's really getting late. They'll think that we're not coming."

They went back through the kitchen. He turned off the kettle, drank some milk, and put his shoes back on. She was dressed totally in black and had a hood on her jacket. He looked at her outfit approvingly.

"You won't be spotted out there at all. If we meet a patrol just stand still or drop to the ground if you can."

She went back through the house to retrieve a backpack she had left in the front hall. He again filled his from his cupboard, and they were off. They left through the back door.

Chapter 31

The dank odor of the field grass exploded into their nostrils with each step. They had made it past the last street undetected and entered the tall grassy field.

A commotion behind them caused them to stop. Dan grabbed at Chrissie and pulled her down with him into the deep grass. Motionless, they waited. A man that they recognized as Norman half ran, half stumbled into their view. He came from the back alley that they themselves had just come from. As they watched, two soldiers appeared at the edge of their vision. One of them dropped to his knees, the other stood straight. Both of them fired a shot from their rifles, and Norman dropped to the ground.

Dan was in a sort of shock. As soon as the soldiers left, he led Chrissie and helped her to follow him. They had already ascertained that Norman was dead. They had watched as the soldiers approached the prostrate figure and shot two more bullets into him.

The moonlight enabled them to make their way across the meadow. Both of them were going as fast as they could. The vegetation brushed against their legs causing some resistance and tiring them. Finally they reached the woods. Once again he led as they moved along the paths that they had so often traveled as kids. She was amazed at how little had changed. Everything was quiet. They got to the entrance without incident, and thanks to the full moon, were able to find their way.

Dan breathed a sigh of relief. He couldn't see Chrissie's face clearly, but he knew that she was terrified.

"We made it!" he exclaimed triumphantly.

"It's strange," she said. "I never thought that I'd feel safe in the woods at night. You're so different tonight; you're not the same Dan that I've grown up with."

She was right! He knew that he wasn't the same. Everything he did was almost spontaneous, automatic, without worrying about possible results. One action led into another, and danger had made a decisive man out of him. No longer did he mull things over. His actions were more of an internal gut reaction to whatever circumstances he was facing.

He didn't answer her charge, instead he said, "We'll be okay now. Those soldiers won't be tramping around in the woods at night. They checked out this area a few days ago. They didn't find the entrance to the cave, and I don't think that they'll be back."

Chrissie was surprised to find out that she knew the way, too. It had all started to come back to her. She was remembering and trying to see the path markers in the dark. There was the rock that signaled a sharp right. Its pale surface stood out in the darkness like a beacon.

"I know the way now!" she exclaimed. As soon as she had spoken out, a little too loudly, they froze. Something came crashing toward them out of the bush. Before the startled pair could move, a gun was pointed at them.

A deep loud voice commanded, "Stop!"

"Let's have the light over here!" was the next command. A bright beam illuminated their faces and they stood, exposed.

Chapter 32

Chrissie was almost shaking with fear. Then they heard a sigh of relief coming from the person who was holding the flashlight. Two men came close and the light revealed Adam and Bruce. "It's me, you guys, Adam. We've been waiting for you to show up. The others are all in the cave. We decided that we should keep a lookout, and if we saw any soldiers getting too close, we'd have to deal with them."

"The trouble is," interrupted Bruce, "we're not trained for any kind of fighting. All I've ever done is high school wrestling. Fortunately, we haven't caught anybody sneaking about that shouldn't be. To tell you the truth, we don't know what we'll do if we should happen to run into anybody."

"What you just did to us was pretty effective, I'll tell you. I'd check my drawers if we weren't in mixed company," said Dan.

Chrissie laughed, "That's for sure. You certainly frightened me."

"We were chosen because we're pretty good hunters, and at least if we have to shoot, we won't likely miss," Adam explained. "I'm not sure that I could kill a man, though."

"Me either," added Bruce.

"I hope that you never have to find out, but let's get to the cave. It's getting late!" commanded Dan.

The foursome made their way to the edge of the woods and carefully scrutinized the area. The span between the tree line and the mineshaft was the last space to be negotiated. Seeing no problems, they sprinted over and into the mine entrance. They replaced the boards in such a way as to make them look untouched, and entered.

When they got to the cranny that led to the cave, they were happy to notice that everything was quiet. One by one, they squeezed through the opening. A black material had been secured over the opening. It was doing a good job of preventing light from showing on the other side. Dan was impressed. When they got inside, they were enthusiastically greeted by what looked to be a lot of people.

Rob came up to them first.

"We're glad to see you," he told them. "We've done a bit while we've been waiting for you. We've been up on the hill above the cave and we've blocked every crack with moss and small pebbles and mortar that just looks like sand."

"It appears so natural that no one is going to discover the cave from above," Jeff said as he came up to them. "We've gotten rid of the former creepy crawly inhabitants and sealed up everything that could let out light."

"Our air supply is coming in from different spots in the shafts and we've blocked every air space with a layer of black cloth, like the cloth over the doorway." Bruce added. "Our water supply is still good, and we can hold out here until we can decide what to do."

"We've even started a makeshift toilet that should do for starters," Rob explained. "Stan is our plumber and sewer man. He's got some good ideas that will take a bit of work and some equipment that we still haven't brought here. All of us will have to work from a list. This is almost like the scavenger hunts that we used to go on."

"I wish this was going to be as carefree as they were," Dan observed.

Chapter 33

"I've made another discovery that might ensure our survival," Dan said. "We don't have to limit ourselves to this cave. These mine tunnels can hook into an old tunnel system that eventually leads into several places. It ends up either in the woods on the other side of town, towards the city, or in an old farmhouse that's in the middle of about two hundred acres of nothing. The most amazing thing is that there is a huge storeroom in the tunnel. It isn't the size of this cave, but it's full of provisions. It was built as a bomb shelter years ago. We'll have the run of the shafts and several escape routes, with a little bit of work. We'll have to break through from one tunnel system into the other, and hide the connection." He told them about the illustrious history of the farmhouse.

Everyone was listening, and there were a lot of murmurs. All of them were surprised to hear about the old house except old George.

"My father was a gambler, and I recall the way my mom got after him when he'd lost. Sometimes he would lose the rent money, and we'd have a hard time. She never did find out where he went. That must have been the place."

"Come on now, let's get down to business," said a voice from the crowd.

We've been busy," said Jeff. "We feel that we could start living in here by the end of this month. We want to put it off as long as possible, though, in order to stash all the supplies that we can. Come on over here! I'll show you what we've collected so far."

People moved aside to make a path so they could make their way to the back of the cave. Dan and Chrissie were surprised. A large amount of goods were stacked in piles on the floor. There were canned items of every type. Blankets, sleeping bags, pillows, and medical supplies were encased in plastic bags. Everything that was easily transported had been lugged here by hand. Rob had brought five rifles, two revolvers, and ammunition from the station. There were bags of items dumped in a heap to the left of the entrance. These were being sorted by a couple of the women.

Dan recognized Karina and Leesa, who was new in town. They were afraid and didn't want to go back and forth and were intending to stay in the cave.

"Those soldiers are always watching," said Karina. "It's getting hard to trust anybody now."

"Yes," added Leesa, "I was just about to tell Greg about the meetings when he said how great the plans for a one-world government were. He feels that it's the answer to all of life's problems. He's not the only one that feels that way, so it's hard to figure out who we can tell. There are only thirty of us."

Four men were sitting in a circle, intent on a piece of paper. They were making a list of who definitely couldn't be trusted. Another group was in the corner, doing the same except their list was of all of the supplies that had to still be brought. The necessary supplies would be allotted to the person that would claim responsibility for procuring them. Rob would be getting most of the larger items, since he could get them partially here in the cruiser. For a while, at least, he was free to patrol the town as if he were still in charge.

The time went quickly, and a few at a time, they left for town.

They were going to have to work out different routes, so that they didn't wear paths from all of their coming and going. Right now, it was enough to reach their houses safely. Jeff left with Chrissie because he lived right next to her.

Chapter 34

Before Dan left, he took one of the lanterns and went to the end of the mine corridor with Rob and Adam. They were surprised to reach it in just a few minutes, but then a cranny was discovered much like their hidden cave opening. They explored the new crack in the wall and were amazed to find another cave. This one was a lot smaller, but from the back wall of this natural opening Rob spotted traces of debris. It may have been left from the attempt that Jo-Anne's father and his men had made when they almost broke into the mine system. That was why their breakthrough attempt had never been discovered. The tunnel itself hadn't been mined. No one had come across the smaller cave. It probably would have been noticed if the company hadn't been forced to shut down.

The next days came and went all too soon. Gradually everything started to fall into place. Dan ran through his shower and dressed hurriedly. He walked to his store and opened up. He learned as much as he could about the army and picked up every tidbit of news from anyone who came in. Cautiously he searched out those who weren't happy about the turn of events. Dan let them know about the meetings. He didn't tell them where they were being held but offered to meet them in the back lane. If anyone was trying to set a trap, at least he would be the only one caught. Their system would be safe. His evenings were still spent in reconnaissance. Their number grew to fifty.

The tunnel from the house had been connected to the small cave. They now had escape routes and living space from the house to the big cave. Food and clothing had been stored. Ventilation was created or reopened. Women were to be bunked in the house with its labyrinth of escapes. There were fifteen of them. The men would be divided between the bunker and the small cave to sleep. Three couples were married, but they decided to go along with the segregated sleeping arrangements until their new way of life underground was established. The large cave would be the main room and the water that formed its own pool would be put to good use.

The whole area had been expertly camouflaged. Not a bit of light showed from outside of the areas they were using. Sounds from the caverns or the storeroom couldn't be heard from the tunnel until the very end. A warning of some kind was going to have to be implemented against anyone coming into the tunnel and catching them unaware.

When the wall had been broken down, Dan led the whole company through the tunnel system. He showed them the storeroom, pointed out the escape that led to the woods, and led them up and into the library. They were all amazed. Jo-Anne and Ashley heard the commotion and joined them.

When Ashley saw Jeff she started, "I never thought that I would see you again."

He was speechless at first sight of her and then he responded. "No, me either. For a long time, I hoped that you would come. At the same time, I didn't want to cause you to give up your job for me."

The smile on his face told her more than any words, but he went on. "I am certainly glad that you're here now. Life has some wonderfully strange twists."

"Don't think that it will always be this easy," Rob addressed the assembly. "So far we've been left alone. The reason is because those soldiers know that there is no real escape. They know that we will eventually die of starvation, thirst, or the need for medicine. They will certainly start looking harder for us when we all suddenly disappear and don't show up for that mark they're planning to give us.

"They searched these areas when they were looking for the children. They didn't give more than a cursory look into the tunnels. We can expect them to come back. I'd like to be ready for them. We may have to block some of the tunnels. If we can do it properly, we can make them think that they're unsafe. Maybe they'll cross them off of their list of places to look for us."

There were murmurs of assent.

"When do we start really living here?" asked Tom.

"I'd like us to keep on bringing things. We'll have to stay here for a long while, and we don't want to run out of food. Just keep lugging survival equipment for a while. Take the big stuff apart, carry a little at a time, and we'll reassemble it here. Make sure that no one sees you. If you run into anyone, go back home for a couple of hours," ordered Dan. "When it's finally time, we'll know it. They'll be threatening to mark us. At the first instruction to gather at the center to be implanted, take off and we'll congregate here."

Chapter 35

In town and in Dan's store, things almost looked normal again. People still came in and had lunch or a coffee. Those with missing family members or kids seemed resigned to not knowing what had happened. Life went on. Money was still being exchanged for goods and services the way it always had. Newspapers were stacked by the front door as they usually were. On his last normal day, as he brought the papers in, he noticed the headlines. A huge blowup of a rather benign-looking man filled half of the front page. He was dressed in a military manner, with medals stretched across his chest in three rows.

The headlines above the picture read, "Peace in the Middle East."

Thanks to the efforts of this charismatic leader, peace has been declared between Israel and all of the Arab nations. The Palestinians have united under their new leader. Concessions and compromises have been made on both sides. Israel is to rebuild their third temple. For the first time in over 2,000 years, Israelites will be able to once again atone for their sins the way that they were commanded to by their God. The Ark of the Covenant has been rediscovered. For all these years, it has been carefully hidden away awaiting its proper resting place.

READY—TO RESIST

A World Religion is being negotiated. Even now the leaders of the churches, mosques, temples, and synagogues are meeting at the Vatican City with the Pope. The rules and belief system will incorporate all of the major religions, and there will be no more confusion or cause for debates.

The Commonwealth of Nations has been unanimous in the vote to appoint this unique man of peace as Governor of the Globe.

Dan put the paper down thoughtfully. That's what the Bible said was going to happen. For three years there really is going to be peace. At the end of the three and a half years; all hell will literally break loose.

This man will sit on the throne in the new temple and declare himself to be God. He will demand to be worshiped, and anyone who will not worship him will be put to death. He will rule over the earth for another three and a half years of horror that will be even worse than the Holocaust.

Jesus Himself will come back to overthrow him and set up His thousand-year reign. This is going to be the last chance for anyone who has never believed in Him.

Dan wanted to have that chance. One condition that was clearly laid out was the fact that no one that had a mark in the hand or forehead would ever be part of the eternal kingdom of God. Never would he allow himself to be marked!

He didn't know what he would say to them. He'd never liked to have anybody preach at him. Regardless of how he felt, all of the people in his group would have to be made to understand. Things that were prophesied so long ago were happening now. Too bad that he hadn't listened to his mom; he'd be gone with all of the others.

What they had to do now was to work undetected from their underground tunnel system. They had to survive and connect with others from other towns and cities. They had to last out the whole seven years, and they had to warn anyone who would listen about the mark. He looked at the new black machine that was sitting on his counter. It was ready to record the computer chip mark that would be on the hand or the forehead of each customer. A cashless society made so much sense that almost everyone would fall for it, and be damned forever.

    He shuddered.